W0270659

# The First Day

Marc Rossignol

# THE FIRST DAY

# *Network*

*Lockdown Wall*

2020, acrylic on canvas, 6 × (89 × 89 cm). Annie Gentils Gallery, Antwerp 2020.

*. Network + $9^2/7^2/5^2$, $Y^2/R^2/B^2$*
2020, acrylic on canvas, 89 × 89 cm

*Network +* $9^2/7^2/5^2$, $Y^2/B^2/R^2$

2020, acrylic on canvas, 89 × 89 cm

*Network 1 source + $9^2/7^2/5^2$, $Y^2/R^2/B^2$*
2020, acrylic on canvas, 89 × 89 cm

*Network + $9^2$ / $7^2$ / $5^2$ / $3^2$*
2020, acrylic on canvas, 89 × 89cm

*Network* $+\times\ 9^2/7^2/5^2,\ Y^2/R^2/B^2\ A$

2020, acrylic on canvas, 110 × 110 cm

*Network +× $9^2/7^2/5^2$, $Y^2/R^2/B^2$ B*

2020, acrylic on canvas, 110 × 110 cm

*Network × 9²/7²/5², Y²/R²/B²*
2019, acrylic on canvas, 89 × 89cm

*Network × $9^2$ / $7^2$ / $5^2$ , $Y^2$ / $R^2$ / $B^2$ C*

2019, acrylic on canvas, 89 × 89 cm

*Network* × $9^2$/$7^2$/$5^2$, $Y^2$/$R^2$/$B^2$ A
2019, acrylic on canvas, 89 × 89 cm

*Network* $\times 9^2/7^2/5^2$, $Y^2/R^2/B^2$ *B*

2019, acrylic on canvas, 89 × 89 cm

*Network +× 30*

2020, watercolour on Steinbach, 20 × 20 cm

*Été indien*

2019, acrylic on canvas, 89 × 89cm

*Automne*

2019, acrylic on canvas, 63 × 63 cm

*Automne*

2019, acrylic on canvas, 89 × 89cm

# *Idayak Kamlam*
# *(Lotus Kolam)*

| | | |
|---|---|---|
| mai 2017 | septembre 2017 | janvier 2018 |
| juin 2017 | octobre 2017 | février 2018 |
| juillet 2017 | novembre 2017 | mars 2018 |
| août 2017 | décembre 2017 | avril 2018 |

*De mai 2017 à avril 2018*

2018, acrylic on canvas, 12 × (42 × 84 cm). Annie Gentils Gallery, Antwerp, 2018.

detail: mai 2017

detail: juin 2017

*De mai 2017 à avril 2018*

2017, acrylic on canvas, 12 × (42 × 84 cm)

*Mai 2017*
2017, acrylic on canvas, 42 × 42 cm

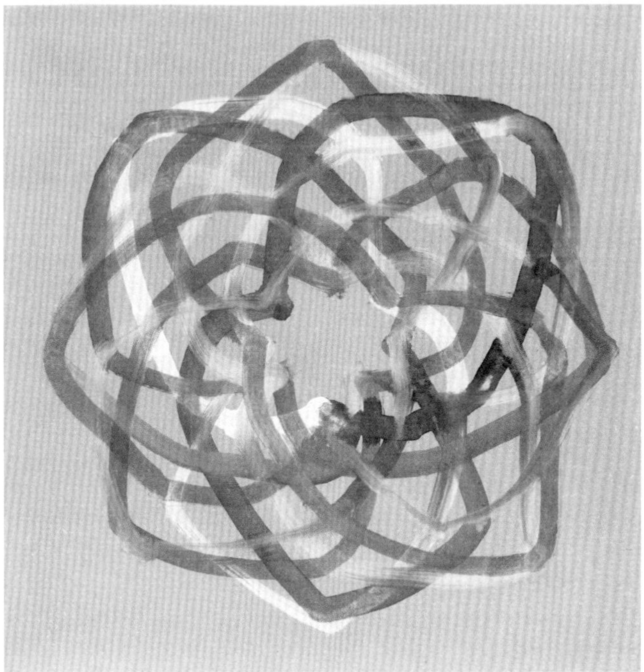

*Juin 2017*
2017, acrylic on canvas, 42 × 42 cm

detail: juillet 2017

detail: août 2017

*De mai 2017 à avril 2018*
2017, acrylic on canvas, 12 × (42 × 84 cm)

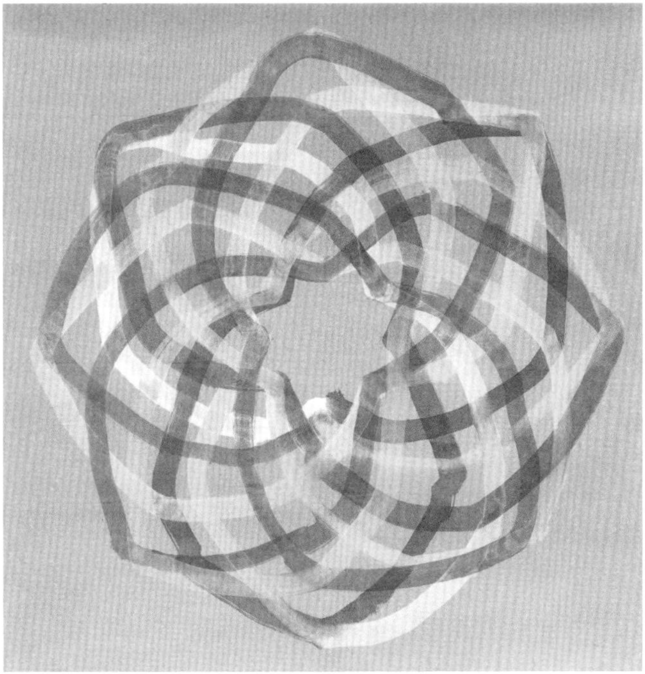

*Juillet 2017*
2017, acrylic on canvas, 42 × 42 cm

*Août 2017*
2017, acrylic on canvas, 42 × 42 cm

detail: septembre 2017

detail: octobre 2017

*De mai 2017 à avril 2018*
2017, acrylic on canvas, 12 × (42 × 84 cm)

*Septembre 2017*
2017, acrylic on canvas, 42 × 42 cm

*Octobre 2017*
2017, acrylic on canvas, 42 × 42 cm

detail: novembre 2017

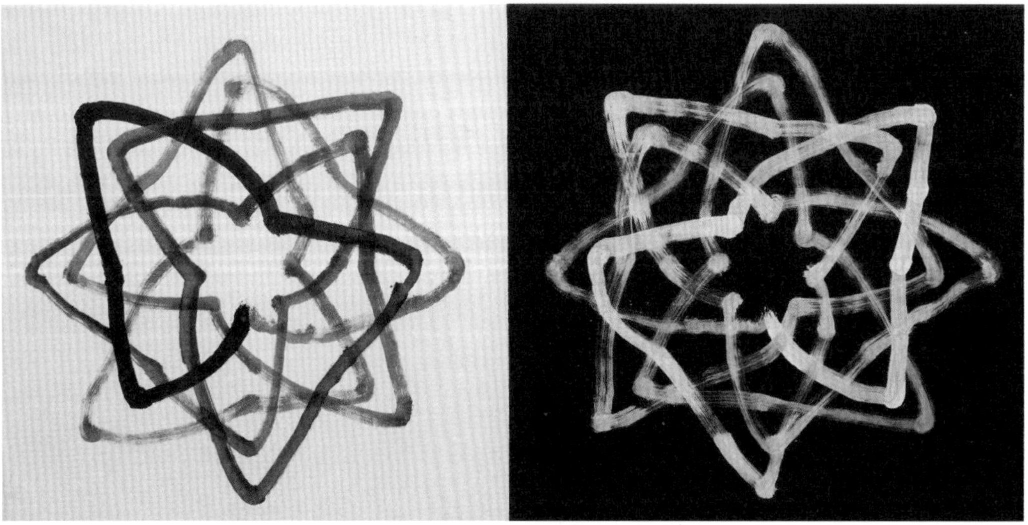

detail: décembre 2017

*De mai 2017 à avril 2018*
2017, acrylic on canvas, 12 × (42 × 84 cm)

*Novembre 2017*
2017, acrylic on canvas, 42 × 42 cm

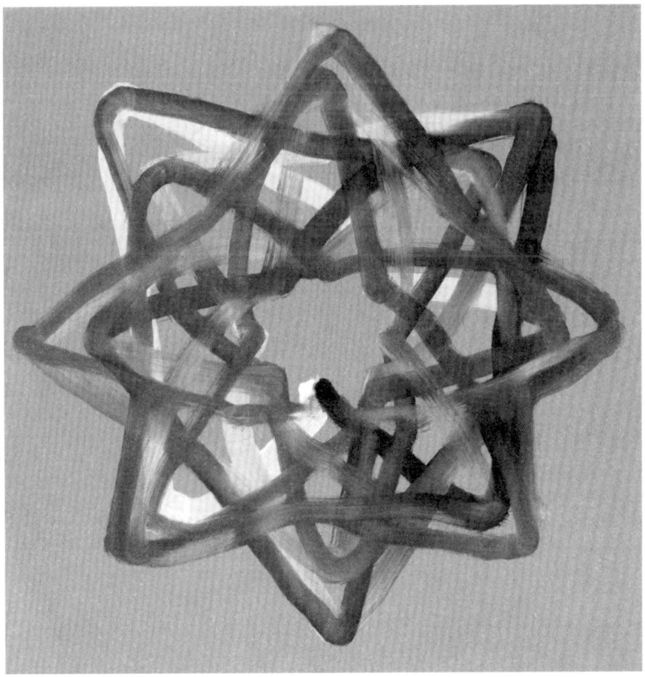

*Décembre 2017*
2017, acrylic on canvas, 42 × 42 cm

detail: janvier 2018

detail: février 2018

*De mai 2017 à avril 2018*
2017, acrylic on canvas, 12 × (42 × 84 cm)

*Janvier 2018*
2018, acrylic on canvas, 42 × 42 cm

*Février 2018*
2018, acrylic on canvas, 42 × 42 cm

detail: mars 2018

detail: avril 2018

*De mai 2017 à avril 2018*
2017, acrylic on canvas, 12 × (42 × 84cm)

*Mars 2018*
2018, acrylic on canvas, 42 × 42cm

*Avril 2018*
2018, acrylic on canvas, 42 × 42cm

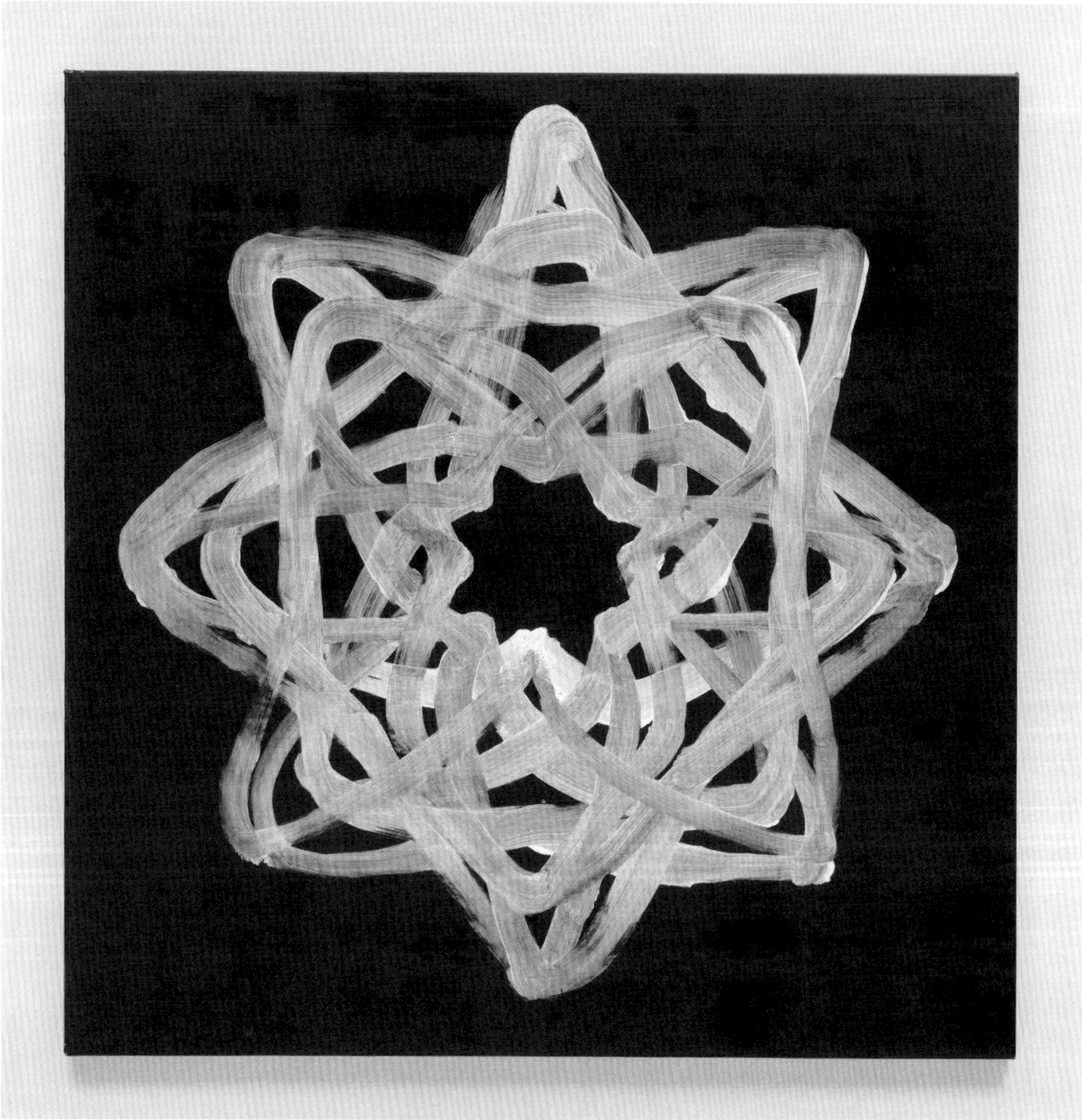

*Janvier 2018*

2018, acrylic on canvas, 110 × 110 cm

*Février 2018*

2018, acrylic on canvas, 110 × 110 cm

*Mars 2018*

2018, acrylic on canvas, 110 × 110 cm

*Avril 2018*

2018, acrylic on canvas, 110 × 110 cm

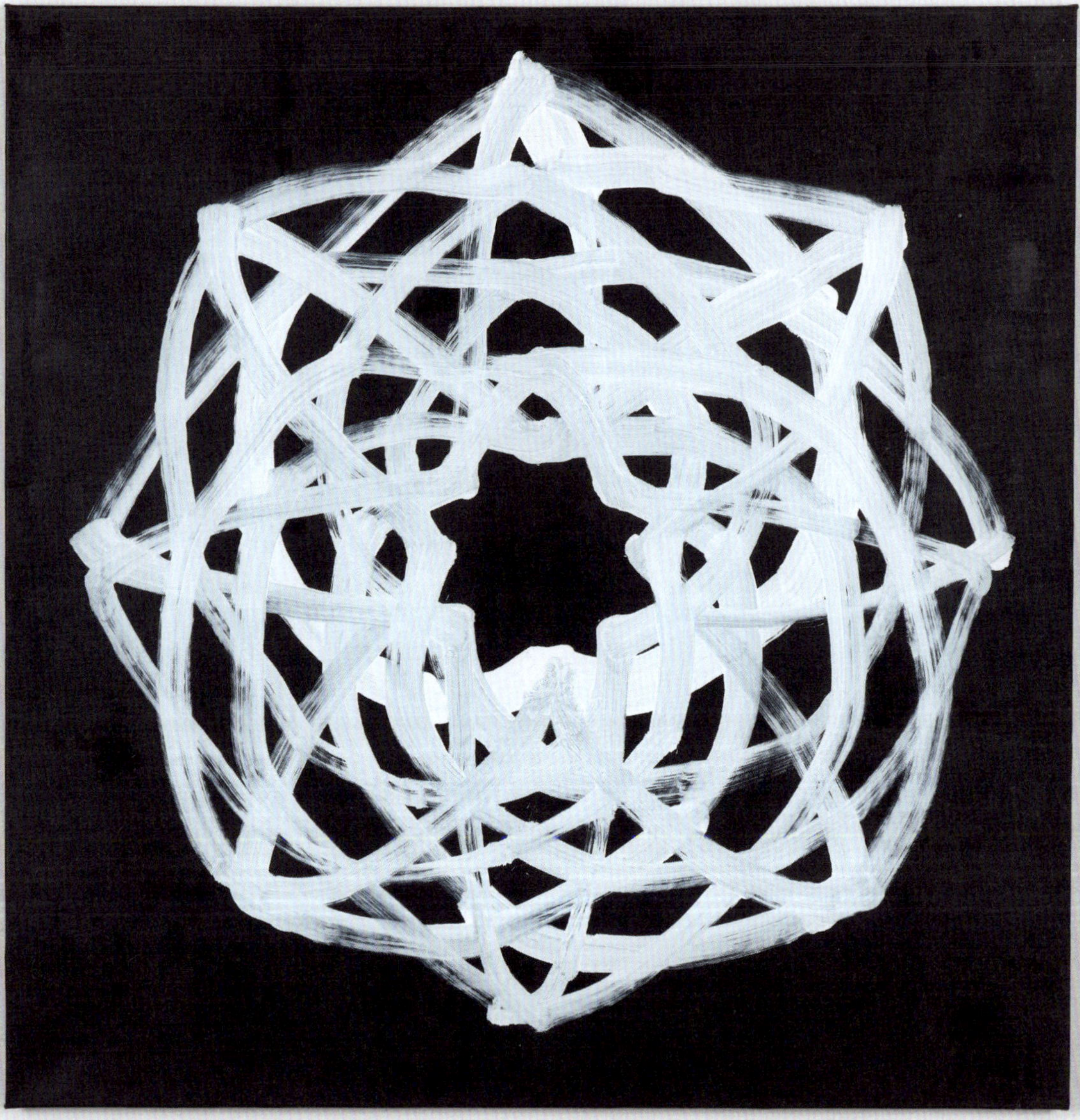

*Mai 2018*
2018, acrylic on canvas, 110 × 110 cm

*Juin 2018*
2018, acrylic on canvas, 110 × 110 cm

*Juillet 2018*

2018, acrylic on canvas, 110 × 110 cm

*Août 2018*

2018, acrylic on canvas, 110 × 110 cm

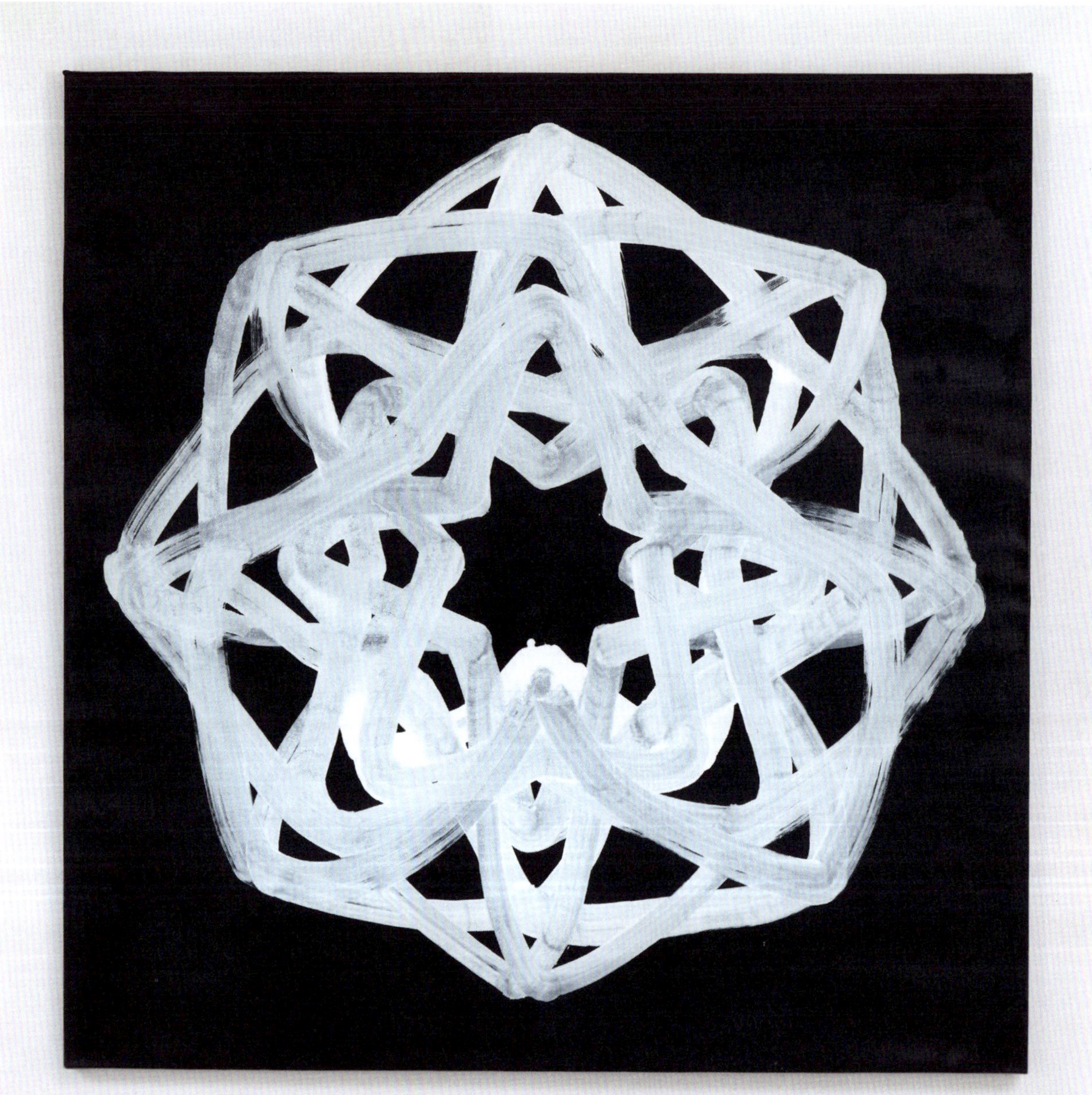

*Septembre 2018*

2018, acrylic on canvas, 110 × 110 cm

*Octobre 2018*

2018, acrylic on canvas, 110 × 110 cm

*Novembre 2018*
2018, acrylic on canvas, 110 × 110 cm

*Décembre 2018*

2018, acrylic on canvas, 110 × 110 cm

*Juillet 2017*
2017, acrylic on canvas, 110 × 110 cm. Annie Gentils Gallery, Antwerp, 2018.

*Juillet 2017*

2017, acrylic on canvas 35 × 35 cm

*Février 2018. Mars 2018. Avril 2018. Mai 2018. Juin 2018. Juillet 2018. Août 2018*
2018, acrylic on canvas, 7 × (30 × 30 cm). Annie Gentils Gallery, Antwerp, 2018.

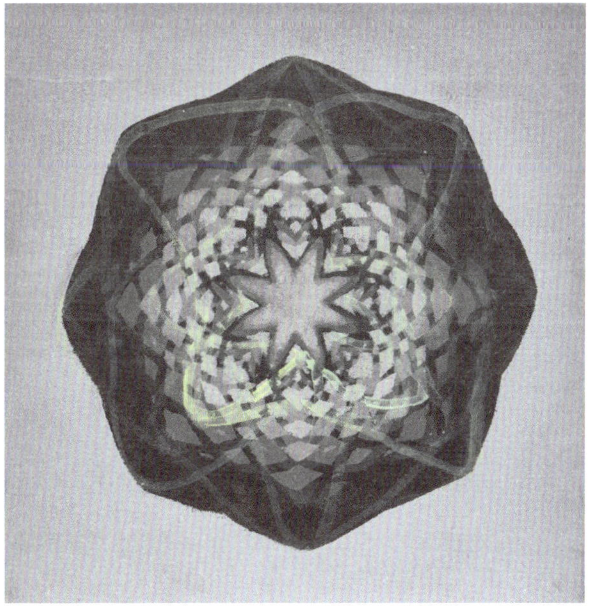

*Janvier 2018*
*Mars 2018*

*Février 2018*
*Avril 2018*

2018, acrylic on canvas, 30 × 30 cm

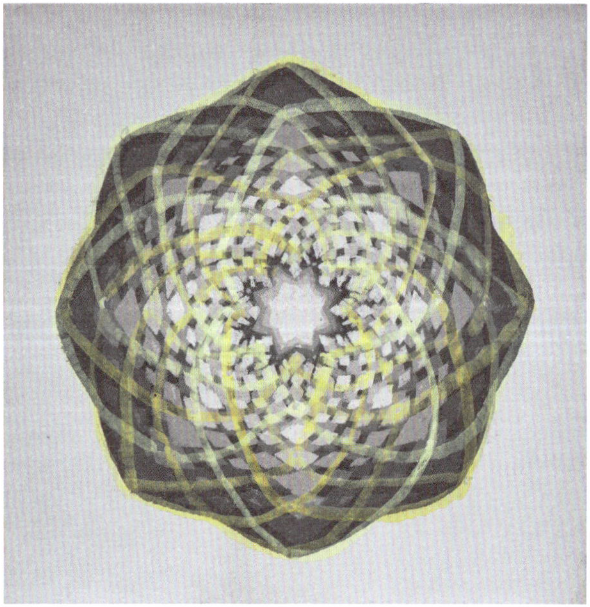

*Mai 2018*
*Juillet 2018*

*Juin 2018*
*Août 2018*



2018, acrylic on canvas, 30 × 30 cm

*Septembre 2018*
*Novembre 2018*

*Octobre 2018*
*Décembre 2018*

2018, acrylic on canvas, 30 × 30cm

*Giverny* and *Juillet 2017*
2016, acrylic on canvas 124 × 75 / 2017, acrylic on canvas 35 × 35. Mu ZEE, Ostend, 2018.

# *Post Monet*

The day following the armistice of the 14–18 war, Monet announced to Clemenceau his intention to donate all of the waterlilies of the Orangerie to the State. The negotiations with the State were well underway in early 1920, since the principle of purchasing of « *Femmes au jardin* », imposed by the artist in exchange for the gift, had at that point been honoured. L'Orangerie was chosen as their permanent location, on the walls of two successive ellipses. The act of the donation was signed in April 1922.

*Sans titre*
2016, acrylic on canvas, 137 × 96 cm

*Post Warhol*

2016, acrylic on canvas, 90 × 90 cm

A work by Warhol, that was painted in the year preceeding his death, is a portrait of a fashion designer named BillyBoy* in the form of a Barbie doll. Most people would have accepted to have their portrait painted by Andy Warhol, but BillyBoy* had always refused. "For many, many, many years he wanted to do a painting of me. And for some reason I didn't appreciate that idea," Billy explains. "Out of annoyance I said to him, 'Well if you really want to do my portrait, do a portrait of Barbie because Barbie, c'est moi.' He took it literally. He took a Barbie that I had given him and turned it into a portrait and called it *Portrait of BillyBoy*."

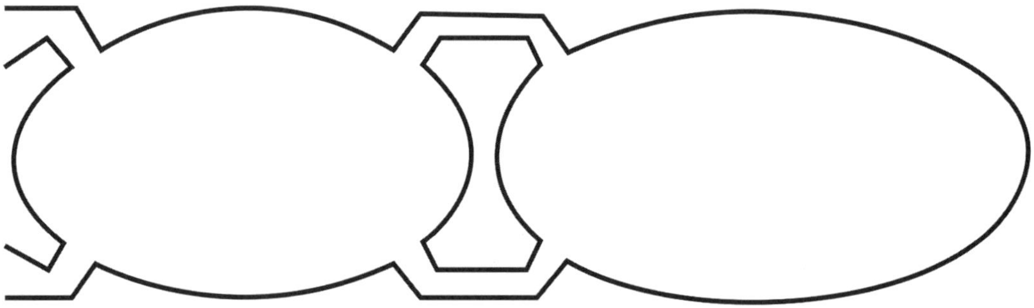



Floor plan of the installation of Monet's *Water Lilies* at the Musée de l'Orangerie Paris.

*Post Monet n° 2*

2017, acrylic on canvas, 96 × 124 + 96 × 135 cm. Annie Gentils Gallery, Antwerp, 2018.

*Post Monet n° 1*

2017, acrylic on canvas, 96 × 124 cm + 96 × 135 cm

*Post Monet n° 3*

2017, acrylic on canvas, 96 × 124 cm + 96 × 135 cm

*Étang*

2017, acrylic on canvas, 100 × 120 cm

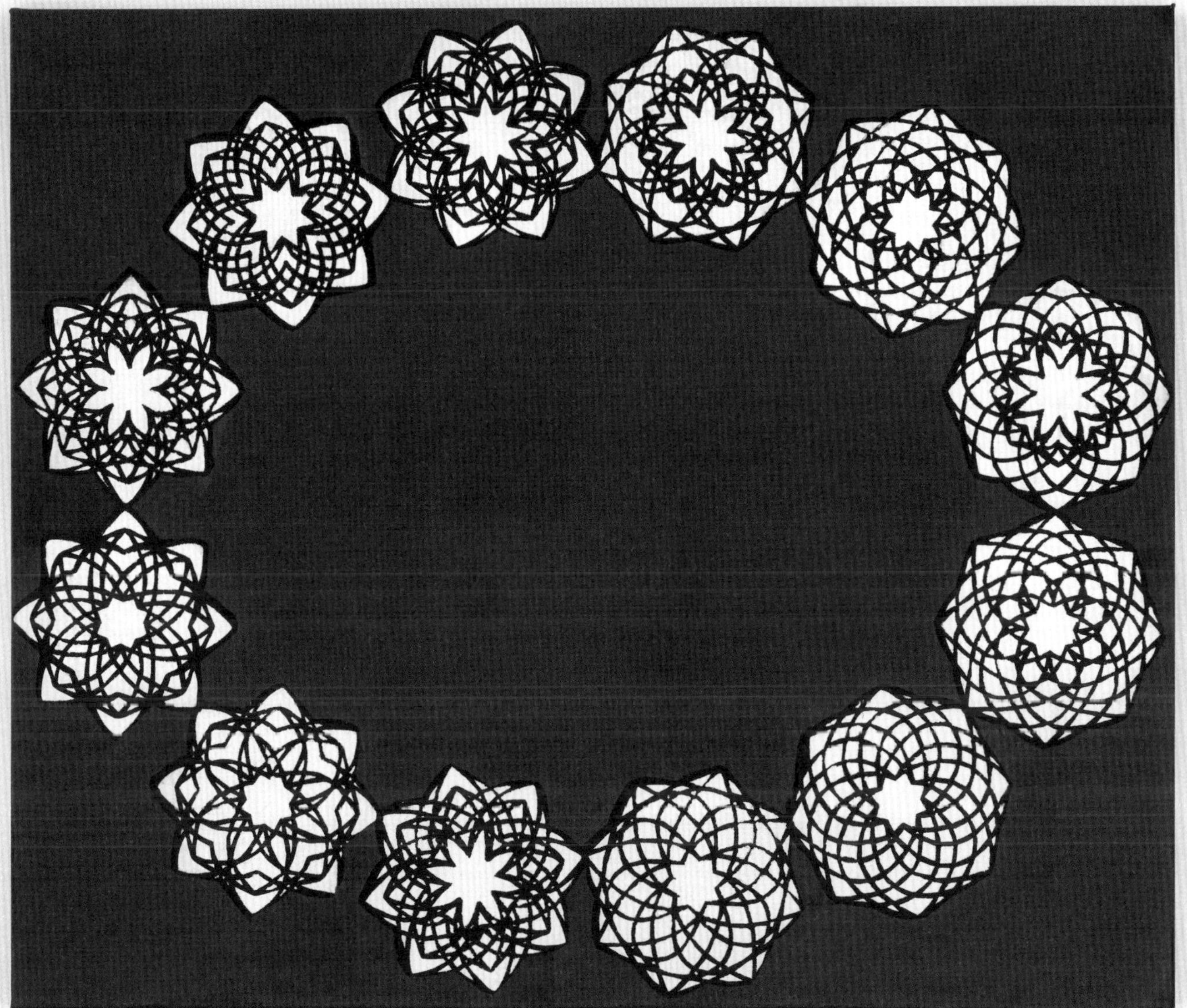

*Constellation*
2017, acrylic on canvas, 100 × 120 cm

*Autour des saisons*
2017, acrylic on canvas, 96 × 124 cm

*Autour des saisons*
2017, acrylic on canvas, 96 × 136 cm

# *Autour des saisons*

*Autour des saisons*
1989, acrylic on canvas, ø 97 cm

*Le tour de l'isle*
1989, acrylic on canvas, 220 × 180 cm

Annie Gentils Gallery, Antwerp, 2018.

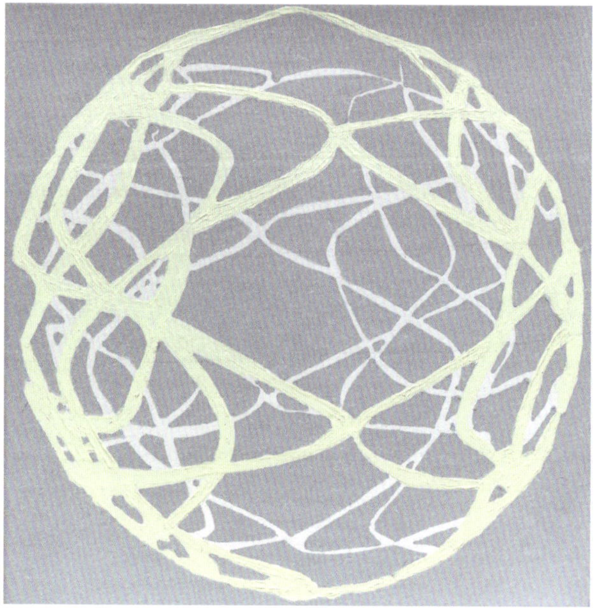

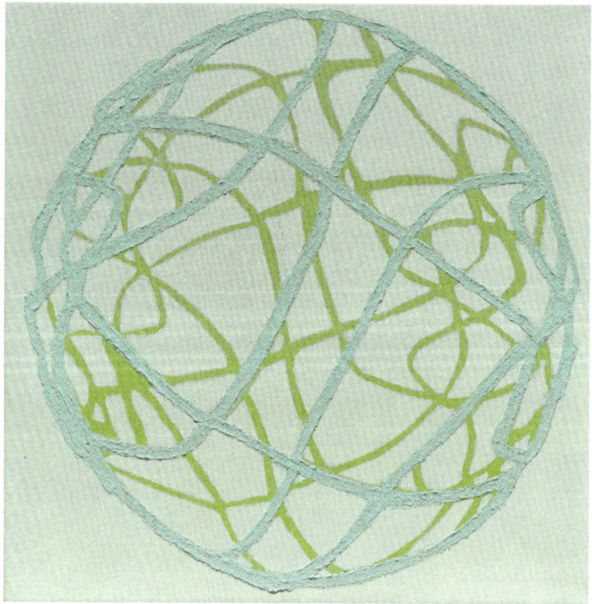

*D'après janvier*
*D'après mars*

*D'après février*
*D'après avril*

2018, acrylic on canvas, 30 × 30 cm

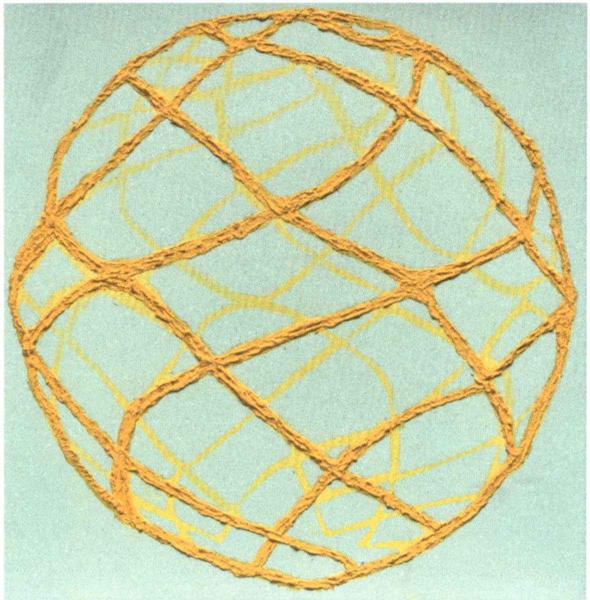

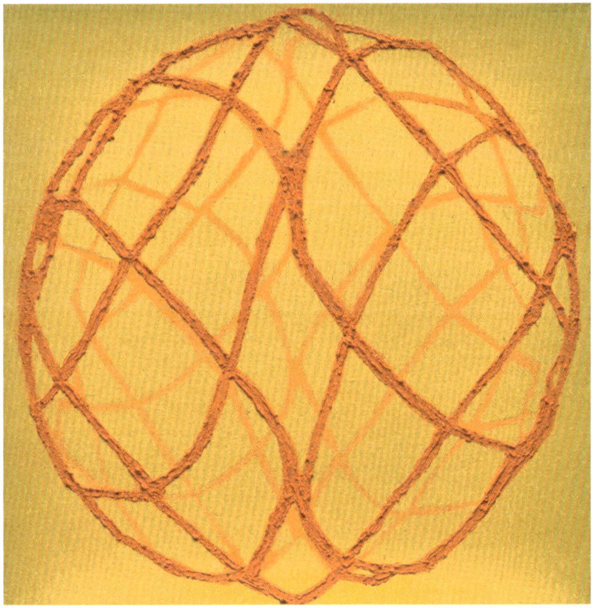

*D'après mai*
*D'après juillet*

*D'après juin*
*D'après août*

2018, acrylic on canvas, 30 × 30 cm

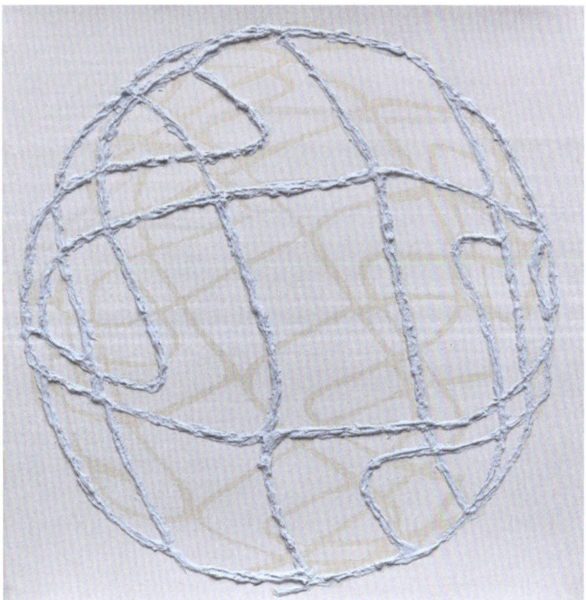

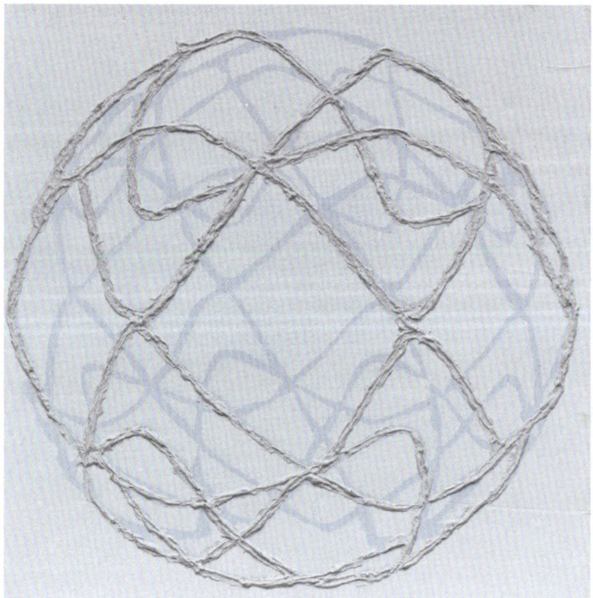

*D'après septembre*
*D'après novembre*

*D'après octobre*
*D'après décembre*

2018, acrylic on canvas, 30 × 30 cm

Annie Gentils Gallery, Antwerp, 2018.

*Bloemen-vogel*

2018, acrylic on canvas, 30 × 180 cm

*D'après janvier*
2018, acrylic on canvas, 89 × 89 cm

*D'après février*
*D'après avril*

*D'après mars*
*D'après mai*

2018, acrylic on canvas, 89 × 89 cm

*D'après juin*
2018, acrylic on canvas, 89 × 89 cm

*D'après juillet*
*D'après septembre*

*D'après août*
*D'après octobre*



2018, acrylic on canvas, 89 × 89 cm

*D'après novembre*
2018, acrylic on canvas, 89 × 89 cm

*D'après décembre*
2018, acrylic on canvas, 89 × 89 cm

# *Lignes continues*

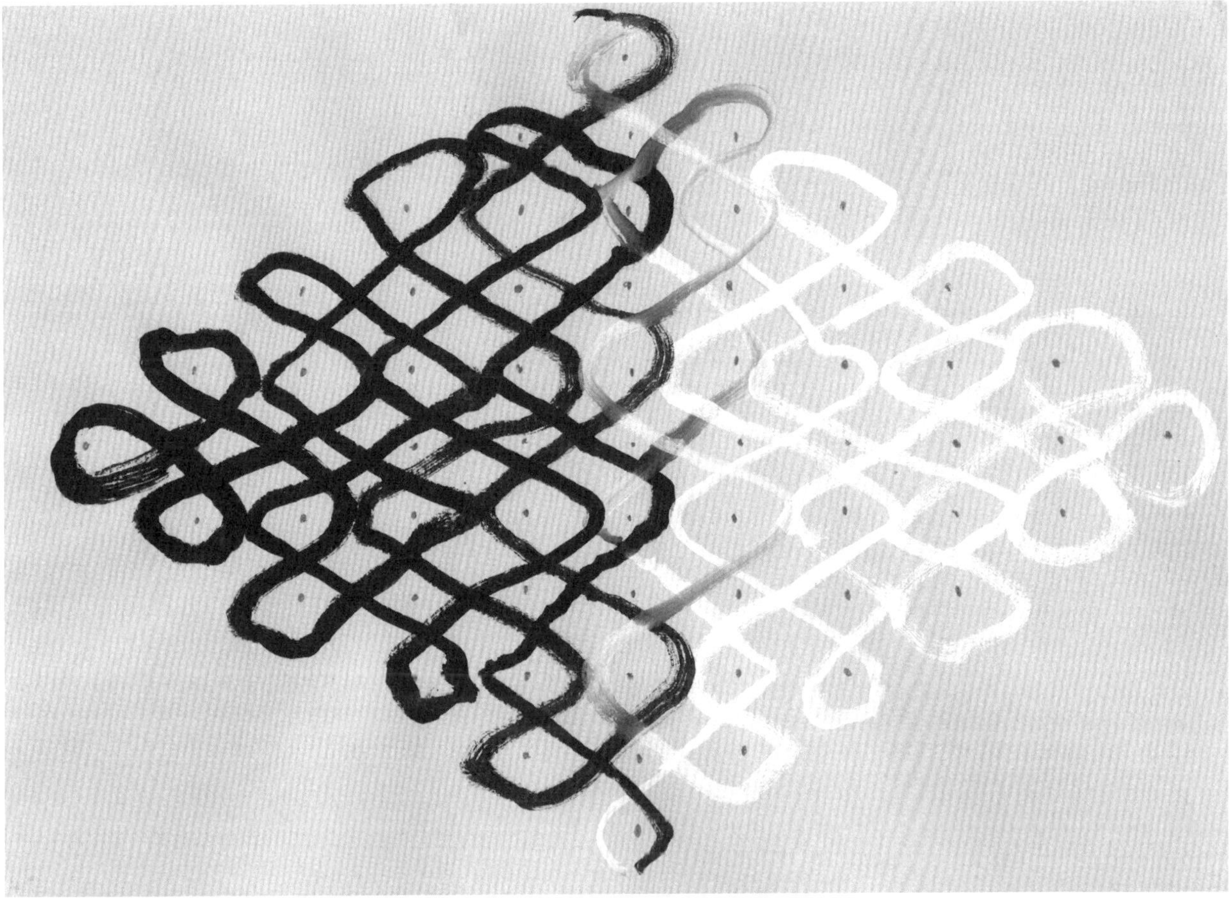

*Appunti per un romanzo sull'imondezza*
2017, acrylic on paper, 21 × 29.7 cm

*Appunti per un romanzo sull'imondezza*
2017, acrylic on paper mounted on canvas, 110 × 110 cm

A.VE.NU.DE.JET.TE — INSTITUT DE CARTON, Brussels, 2017.

*Obélisque d'axoum*
2011, acrylic on canvas, 7 × (20.5 × 110 cm)

*Collier de la reine 4*
2008, acrylic on canvas, 140 × 109cm

*Noeud 2*

2007, acrylic on canvas, 84 × 67 cm. Sofam, Brussels, 2018.

*Rézo zéro 3*

2007, acrylic on canvas, 67 × 67 cm

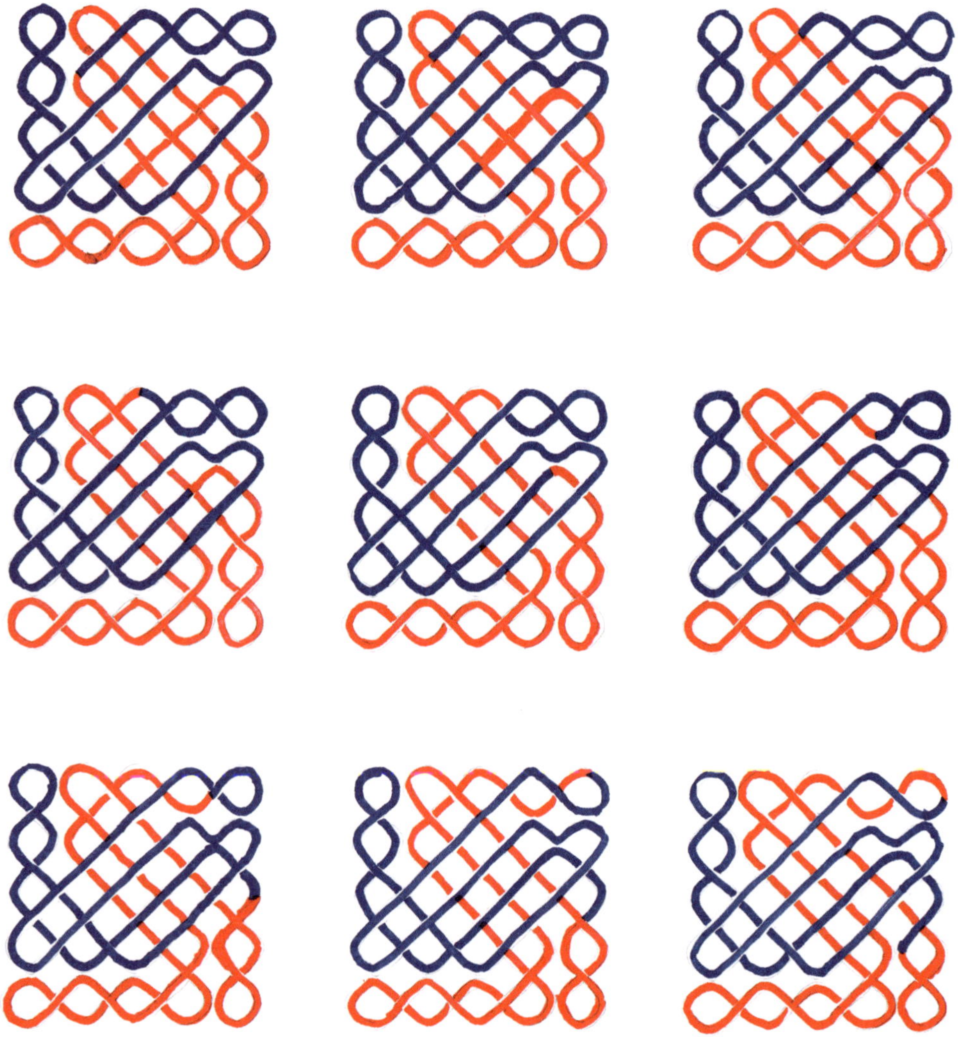

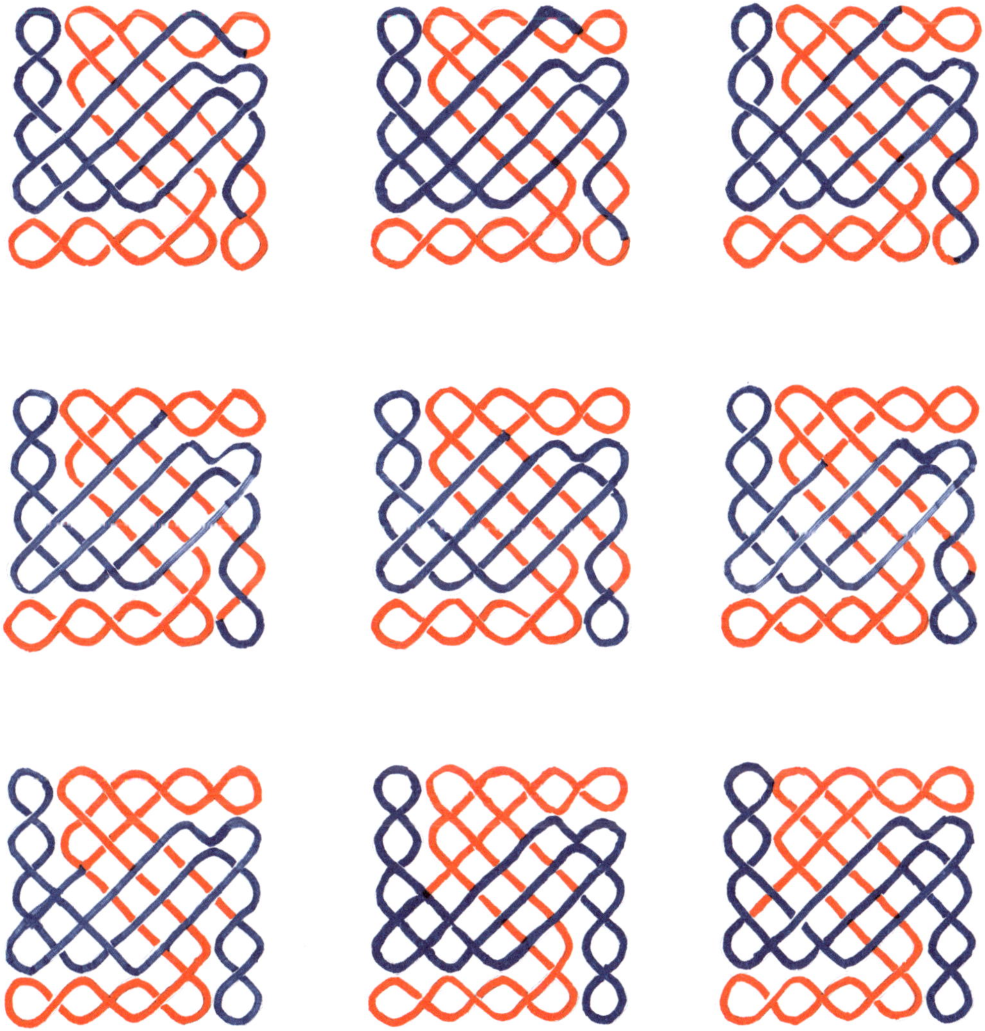

*Main eau coeur*

2009, marker on paper for an animation film (18 of 100), 21 × 29 cm

*Nuage*

2007, plastic, 25 × 335 × 45 cm. Sofam, Brussels, 2018.

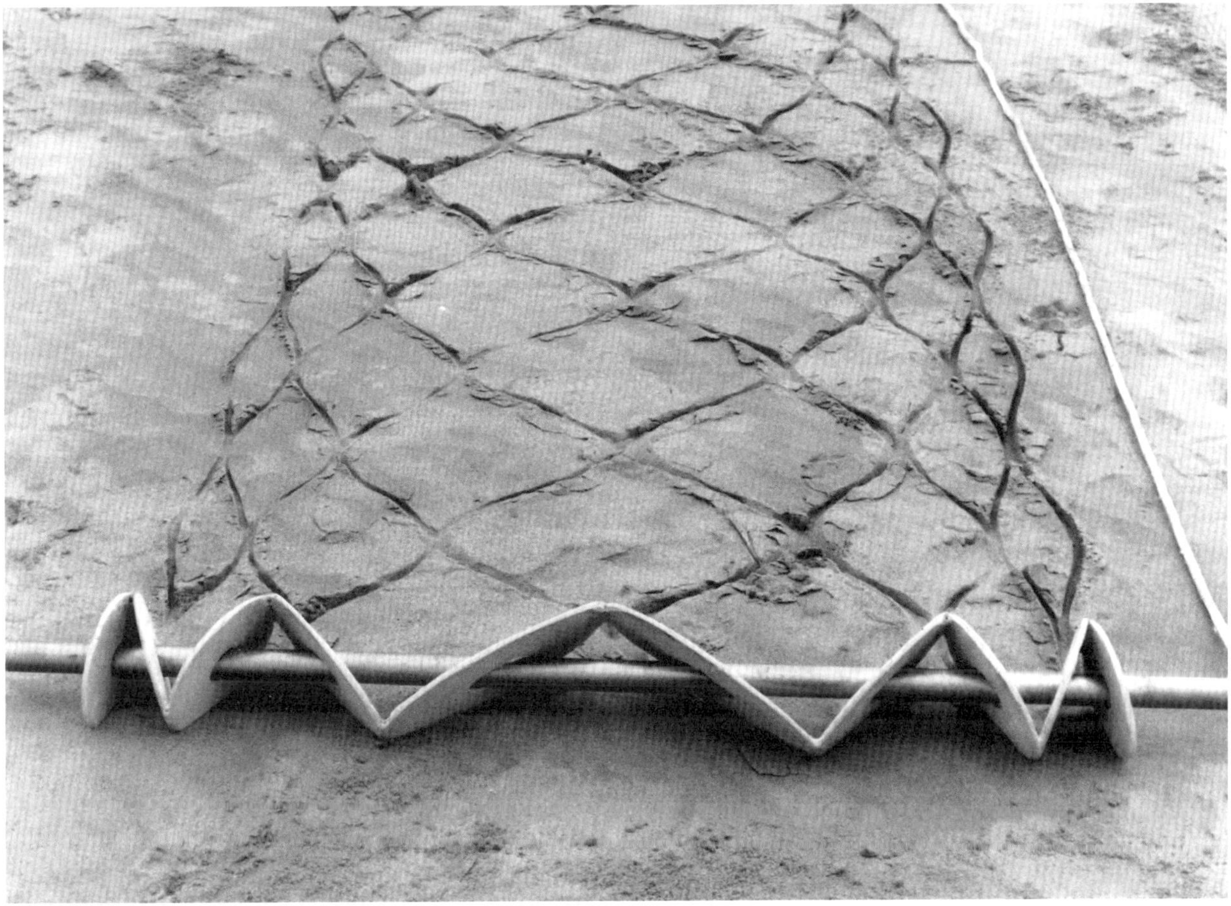

*Serpent de mer*
1995, polyester, 120 × 18 × 18 cm

Maison de la Culture, Namur, 2008.

Middelkerke, 2000.

# *Performances*

*(Roue de trois)*
Het Groene Labyrint, Westerlo, 1999.

*Alphabets*

Les Halles de Schaerbeek, Brussels, 2004.

Sand drawings, Venice, 2009.

*Le chant des âmes retrouvées*
Galerie Vincenz Sala, Paris, 2013.

*Le chant des âmes retrouvées*
A.VE.NU.DE.JET.TE – INSTITUT DE CARTON, Brussels, 2017.

*Le premier jour*

With Laetitia Yalon, Maison de la culture, Namur, 2017.

*Drawing on the wall*
S.M.A.K., Ghent, 2010.

To mark the opening of the European House of the Authors in Spring 2018, SOFAM invited visual artist Marc Rossignol in Brussels, to carry out his performance *Le Premier Jour*. During this painting-in-action, named after a poem by Edouard Glissant, Rossignol paints 12 kolams, one for each month, with a large brush in each hand, painting symmetrically and in mirror image, whilst at the same time reciting each of the twelve verses of Edouard Glissant's poem. This complex task is aided by the specific shapes of the kolams and the words of the poem which reinforce the artist's memory of each. And so these two cultural artefacts serve in the creation of something entirely new.

Kolams are generally made up of one continuous line that passes over an arrangement of points. These intricate geometric designs originate from matriarchal societies in Southern India. The drawings are, still today, drawn with rice powder on the pavement in front of the home: it is believed the design invites the gods to look on them favourably. By evening, the feet passing over them disperse the drawings. A new one is painted the following morning. The closed patterns were also believed to emprison evil spirits, so they would be prevented from entering the house.

Marc Rossignol is interested in their geometry, the application of mathematics – which he calls *Mathématique Pathétique*, since it is mathematics at the service of poetry and sacred rites, rather than its sole application in the developed world, where it is mostly used for homogenisation and profit. Whilst he admits he is not capable of believing in the magic, which was at the origin of all mathematics, the poetry remains and he postulates this in his work as an alternative, symbolic currency.

Kate Christina Mayne

*De eerste dag*
With Kurt Du Tré, Annie Gentils Gallery, Antwerp, 2018.

# DE EERSTE DAG

*Phillip Van den Bossche*

Deze zinnen over Marc Rossignols artistieke praktijk vormen niet meer dan een begin, alsof zijn kunstwerken uitnodigen om een nieuw gebied van de wereld op te zoeken. Een nieuw gebied dat bovendien verre van onbekend is, maar door de tijd en de manier waarop beeldende kunst zich in het Westen heeft ontwikkeld, wel zo goed als vergeten. Van het laatste schilderij van een kunstenaar terug naar een begin, van een eindpunt naar een startpunt: onderweg vinden we verschillende 'kunstgeschiedenissen' maar ook de slavernij en het imperialisme. De geschiedenis van de representatie valt ermee samen: zowel de zogenaamde autonomie van het geschilderde als het collectief gedeelde en ervaren gegeven tegenover datgene wat het representeert. Het samengaan van rite, handeling, het orale, woord en beeld, ambacht en kunst, wereld en mens waren we samen met onze koloniale geschiedenis vergeten.

Het is een herwerkte eerste alinea van een korte toespraak die ik op 23 december 2017 gaf, naar aanleiding van de Prijs Bernd Lohaus. We zijn drie jaar verder en deze publicatie draagt de titel van een gedicht van Édouard Glissant, dichter en filosoof geboren in 1928 op het eiland Sainte-Marie, een gemeente op Martinique. De tentoonstelling en de uitreiking kreeg toen een onderkomen bij A.V.E.NU.DE.JET.TE - INSTITUT DE CARTON — een straatnaam in stukken verknipt door een 'instituut in karton', het paste toen en het vloeit nog altijd wonderwel samen met mijn kennismaking, pas een half jaar eerder, met Marc Rossignols artistieke praktijk. Hij gebruikte een montage van sensaties en denkbeelden over het schilderen in relatie tot het lichaam waar geen consensus over bestaat. Zo probeer ik het vandaag te verwoorden. Toen in december 2017 was ik ook voor de eerste keer getuige van een van zijn performances: hij schilderde tegelijkertijd met zijn linker- en rechterhand, twee lange penselen in de hand, een identiek gespiegeld motief kreeg vorm met rode en blauwe verf. De handeling van het schilderen ging gepaard met het declameren van een gedicht, *Le chant des âmes*, van François Cheng (1929). De tekening en het motief waren ontleend aan de Tchokwé uit Angola. Het is een 'sona', een in het zand getekende tekening verbonden aan initiatieriten. Samen met Marc Rossignol deelden we tijdens de performance eenzelfde ruimte, zonder het daarom met elkaar eens te zijn over alles, verre van of allesbehalve. Meer nog, we deelden de tijd van het schilderen en van het gedicht — niet meer dan een interval, maar daarin ligt net de kracht — eenzelfde plaats en ruimte, een door de performance gecreëerde tijd om heel even samen een kloof te dichten.

Zes maanden eerder in zijn atelier had ik iets gelijkaardigs meegemaakt (zonder het toen te beseffen en vooral het onder woorden te kunnen brengen). De ik-vorm is hier belangrijk om de aandacht te vestigen op een persoonlijke ervaring en een poging tot beschrijving van een kunstwerk en vooral een gedachtegang binnen een oeuvre. En misschien ook, om te wijzen hoe een persoonlijke ervaring iets is wat ons nu in deze pandemietijd door talloze restricties collectief wordt ontnomen.

Een ontmoeting met kunst staat altijd los van instituten en musea, een altaar is altijd sterker dan een muur. Kunst is noch een altaar noch een ideologische muur – al zien we vanuit een conservatieve reflex wel het omgekeerde weer gebeuren. Op 30 augustus werd ik 's ochtends in Brussel-Zuid door Stella Lohaus en Annie De Decker met de auto opgehaald. We gingen een dag lang samen op atelierbezoek naar aanleiding van de Prijs Bernd Lohaus – de namen van de verschillende kunstenaars die we samen zouden ontmoeten, hadden ze me niet doorgegeven. Het eerste atelierbezoek was bij Marc Rossignol. Ik herinner me een langwerpig atelier, koffie, sigaretten, kleine mini-boekjes en speculaaskoekjes, een gesprek ook over Afrikaanse spoken (ons gedeeld koloniaal verleden maar vooral een passie voor de vormen en een ambacht dat nog altijd niet wordt herkend). De splitsing tussen kunst en ambacht valt samen met de slavernij. Hier was geen gesprek over modernisme, wel over het schilderen als een dagelijkse praktijk. Marc Rossignol ontvouwde die ochtend een meterslange rol met geometrische vormen, een Indische 'kolam', wederom simultaan met de linker- en rechterhand geschilderd. Aan de muur, of was het een deur, hing een blad met daarop het gedicht van Glissant (1928–2011). Ik vroeg hem of hij me de tekst wilde doorsturen. Het was het gedicht *Le premier jour*. Samen werden ze een nieuwe perfomance, waar Marc Rossignol vertelde: "Je dessine douze figures déduites d'un kolam indien, nomme « Idayak kamlam », fleur de lotus. Cette performances est plus largement encore en relation avec le temps d'avant le temps, le temps indifférencié, réservoir de tous les possibles." [1]

1 Marc Rossignol, e-mailbericht aan de auteur, 11 mei 2021.

Niemand heeft ooit zo verhelderend over het beeldend werk van Romare Bearden (1911–1988) geschreven als hijzelf. Stileren, in vorm brengen, is de basis van het menselijke bewustzijn en het beginpunt van geschiedenis. Geschiedenis gaat altijd over patronen. Ik parafraseer hier de woorden van de schrijver en jazzcriticus Albert Murray. Ze brengen me terug naar Marc Rossignol, hoe hij een performance benadert als de overgang van ritueel naar kunst. Het spel en de mens. Het ritueel visualiseert de metafoor. Doen deze woorden duizelen? "Once you get into art, you are into vertigo." Marc Albert Murray Rossignol. Albert Marc Rossignol Murray. De wereld is een schilderij.

Het klinkt te heroïsch, als ik het nu herlees – het betreft wederom een paragraaf uit de toespraak. Toen in 2017, was ik de teksten van de muziekcriticus, essayist en schrijver

Albert Murray (1916–2013) aan het lezen. En toch, de duizeligheid blijft al is de wereld misschien geen schilderij, een canvas waarop zomaar alles geprojecteerd kan worden. Wat me tot vandaag boeit is de relatie tot het ritueel van het schilderen bij Marc Rossignol. De aandacht voor de doorvloeiende rol van het creëren, delen en doorgeven.

Het 'duizelen' komt niet uit de lucht vallen, en misschien verwonderlijk, het gebruik van dit woord heeft niet zozeer met het kijken naar de schilderijen van Marc Rossignol te maken. Of nog beter, het betreft hier niet een effect of een gevolg van het kijken. Van kunst terug naar ritueel, dat komt meer in de buurt. De verbinding tussen kunst maken en de oorsprong van rituelen is nog een andere manier om deze gedachtegang verder te zetten.

Wat als we kunst (opnieuw) benaderen vanuit een meer antropologische (en daarom nog niet een eenzijdig Westerse) visie? Albert Murray is hier opnieuw aan het woord: "Another more anthropological definition of art is an elegant extension, celebration, and refinement of the rituals which re-enact survival technology. When you look at a painting, what you see is a stylization, but it is also a visual or plastic re-enactment of a ritual, and a ritual is a ceremonial re-enactment of some aspect of the basic survival techniques of a given cultural configuration, which may be an aboriginal tribe or a very highly developed nation, a subcontinent, or even a whole continent."[2]

2 Albert Murray, *Collected Essays and Memoirs*. New York: The Library of America, 2016, 895.

Marc Rossignol vertelt met een glimlach na een performance aan een interviewer: "Ik zou willen dat Krishna ons vandaag had beschermd tegen het slechte weer en de regen, maar 'je suis trop pagan'." Het spel, wel of niet betekenis geven aan regels en door het Westen gedicteerde kunstvoorschriften. Als we durven verder kijken bestaat er misschien een groter raffinement aan opties en benaderingen. Albert Murray verwijst niet alleen naar een performatief aspect, maar legt de nadruk op het steeds opnieuw creëren, presenteren en produceren. Van ritueel naar een speelse manier van opnieuw creëren, inclusief improvisatie, persoonlijke keuzes voor bepaalde stijlvormen en elegantie.

Édouard Marc Glissant Rossignol. *Une nouvelle région du monde* is de titel van een boek van Édouard Glissant. Marc Rossignol heeft het me in het najaar van 2017 in de handen gestopt – inclusief een verwijzing naar bepaalde passages en bladzijden: Marc Édouard Rossignol Glisssant. "Le langage dessine et colorie d'abord, *et récite ensuite*", staat op pagina 31. Glissant verhaalt over de oorsprong van taal én van het schilderij, hoe elk boek en elk schilderij of elke representatie, zichzelf oplegt om, in het onderweg zijn, het moment te nemen en te verrassen: "Le tableau, le tableau peint, est (...) un isolat, une halte, une citation de détails, dont on sélectionne volontiers le détail, et c'est tant pis pour la synthèse éclairante (...)."[3] De wereld is een representatie, is een schilderij. Laten we dan terug de duizeling van ontelbare lichtvariaties, de schaduwwerking in grotten, het ritme en de

3 Édouard Glissant, *Une nouvelle région du monde*. Esthétique I. Paris: Gallimard, 2006, 31.

chaos van het universum, met zijn moleculaire structuren en energiebronnen, opzoeken. De anonimiteit van een verloren tijd, verenigd in diversiteit en meervoudigheid, brengt ons misschien naar een nieuw gebied, "voir une esthétique nouvelle, celle peut-être de l'*autre région du monde* que voici là, tout ici." [4]

4
Ibid., 37.

Ik blader terug in Marc Rossignols zelf-uitgegeven miniboekjes en opnieuw zijn er de patronen, reproducties van eerder gerealiseerde kunstwerken, als tegels en abstracte geometrische formaties. Het logo van de Franse krant *Libération* uitgeknipt, de vrijheid als logo vermenigvuldigd tot een nieuwe compositie, cijfers, een eikenblad en *Le Monde*. In 2021 komt het vreemd over dat krantennamen nog 'grote woorden' als titel (blijvend) durven gebruiken. Misschien is het vooral vreemd om dit nu binnen de journalistiek, de zogenaamde vierde macht, te moeten vaststellen. De Franse filosoof Jacques Rancière (1940) zegt hierover: "Il y a toute une série de jeux de langage au cœur de la parole politique qui ont remplacé les grands mots d'ordre sur des banderoles ou dans les haut-parleurs d'antan. L'activisme politique a pris un tour qui le rapproche de certaines formes d'intervention artistique. Par conséquent, chacun vient avec sa propre pancarte, son propre mot d'ordre. C'est vraiment très visible depuis une dizaine d'années. Cela fait partie de la sensibilité du temps. On refait une expérience de monde en dehors des grandes synthèses, à partir de bribes qui sont partagées avec l'art. On pourrait dire qu'on fait aujourd'hui de la politique comme Godard faisait du cinéma il y a cinquante ans." [5]

5
Jacques Rancière, 'L'enjeu est de parvenir à maintenir du dissensus', Jean-Marc Lalanne, in *Les Inrockuptibles*, 15 février 2021, geraadpleegd op 10 mei 2021, https://www.lesinrocks.com/cheek/rencontre-avec-jacques-ranciere-lonjeu-est-de-parvenir-a-maintenir-du-dissensus-157314-15-02-2021/

Tegelijkertijd denk ik dan terug aan wat Marc Rossignol schrijft: "J'étudie dans ce travail un kolam, un dessin que les femmes tracent dans le sud de l'Inde devant leurs portes, au sol avec de la farine de riz pour conjurer le mauvais sort." En niet onbelangrijk wat hij daaraan toevoegt: "Celui que j'ai choisi est un tracé continu et monolinéaire." We hebben het hier niet over fotografie of cinema, die ons de waarheid toont, 24 keer per seconde.

Terug naar de relatie tussen kunst, het dagelijks leven en rituelen, in een ander miniboekje van Marc Rossignol met als titel *Vie et mort de Cézanne, le contexte* lees ik: "L'artiste moderne en devenir, le paysage et la colonisation de l'Algérie". Daarna volgt een gedetailleerde biografie dat in geen enkel museum of archief als geheel terug kan worden gevonden. Want als je historisch perspectief vooral door een tekende hand wordt gestuurd, krijg je een ander verhaal met transculturele dwarsverbanden. Het begin of de eerste fase is vanuit een bepaald oogpunt misschien onbestemd. Het gaat om de mogelijkheid om 'in' en 'door' contexten te navigeren. Ik denk aan een veren hoofddeksel, een pagode, een wigwam, een hut, een auto, een sfinx, weefsels, een windmolen, een kasteel, piramides, een flatgebouw, een nieuw weefsel, een ziggoerat, een hut, een grotwoning, een berggedeelte en steeds opnieuw is er een weefsel en patronen. Want de schoonheid, "tussen de dag en zijn vuurzee", ligt steeds weer open, waar dan ook. [6]

6
Édouard Glissant, *Le sel noir*. Paris: Editions du Seuil, 1960. Origineel in het Frans en de laatste zin uit het gedicht *Le premier jour*, vertaald door de auteur: 'Parmi le jour et son embrasement'.

# THE FIRST DAY

*Phillip Van den Bossche*

These lines on Marc Rossignol's artistic practice are no more than a point of entrance, as if his artworks are an invitation to venture into a new region of the world. He beckons us into a region that is moreover far from unknown, but which, due to the passage of time and the way the fine arts developed in the West, has been all but forgotten. From an artist's latest painting back to a beginning, from an ending to a starting point: along the way we find various 'art histories' but also slavery and imperialism.  The history of representation coincides with this: both the so-called autonomy of what is painted, and the collectively shared and experienced situation that stands opposite what it is representing. Along with our colonial history, we had forgotten the convergence of ritual, action, the oral, word and image, craft and art, the world and the human being.

The above is a reworked opening paragraph of a short speech I gave on the 23rd of December 2017, on the occasion of the Bernd Lohaus Prize. Three years later, this publication bears the title of a poem by Édouard Glissant, the poet and philosopher born in 1928 on the island of Sainte-Marie, a municipality of Martinique. The exhibition and award ceremony took place at A.V.E. NU.DE.JET.TE – INSTITUT DE CARTON — a street name that is chopped into pieces by a 'cardboard institution'. It was appropriate at the time and aligned beautifully with my acquaintance, six months previously, with Marc Rossignol's artistic practice. He used a montage of sensations and mental imagery regarding painting in relation to the body, a practice that elicited multiple responses. This is how I attempt to verbalize it today. Then, in December 2017, I was privy, for the first time, to one of his performances: he painted simultaneously with his left and right hand, wielding two long paintbrushes, one dipped in red paint and the other in blue paint. The act of painting was coupled with the recital of a poem, *Le chant des âmes*, by François Cheng (1929). The drawing and motif were borrowed from the Chokwe in Angola. It is a 'sona', a drawing in the sand connected to rites of initiation. Together with Marc Rossignol we shared the same space during the performance, without therefore having to agree on everything, far from it. More than that, we shared the time of the painting and the poem — no longer than an interval, but therein lies its very power — the same space and time, a timespan created by the performance, in which to momentarily bridge a divide.

I had experienced something similar in his studio six months earlier (without realising it at the time and, especially, being unable to put it into words). The first-person singular is important here, to draw attention to a personal experience, and an attempt to describe an artwork and especially an enduring suite of mental processes within an oeuvre. And perhaps also, to accentuate how a personal experience is something that has now been collectively taken from us through countless restrictions during these pandemic-affected times.

An encounter with art is always separate from institutions and museums: an altar is always way more powerful than just a wall. Art is neither an altar nor an ideological wall — even though we can see the opposite impulse arise once more, driven by a conservative reflex. On the 30th of August I was picked up at Brussels' South station by Stella Lohaus and Annie De Decker. We were going to spend the day together, to do studio visits on the occasion of the Bernd Lohaus Prize. They had not given me the names of the various artists we were going to visit. The first studio visit was with Marc Rossignol. I remember an oblong studio, coffee, cigarettes, small mini publications and *speculoos* biscuits: a conversation, too, about African ghosts (our shared colonial past, but especially a passion for forms and crafts that are still underrecognized). The split between art and craft coincided with the advent of slavery. Here was no conversation about modernism: the talk was about painting as a daily practice. Marc Rossignol unrolled a meters-long scroll of geometric forms, an Indian 'kolam', again painted simultaneously using both hands. On the wall, or was it a door, there hung a piece of paper with the poem by Édouard Glissant (1928–2011). I asked him whether he would like to send me the text. It was the poem *Le Premier Jour* ('The First Day'). Together, these elements became a new performance, about which Marc Rossignol said: 'I draw twelve figures derived from an Indian kolam, named "idayak kamlam", lotus flower. In a larger sense, this performance stands in relation to the time before time, undifferentiated time, the reservoir of all possibilities." [1]

Nobody wrote in a more enlightening manner about Romare Bearden's work (1911–1988) than Romare Bearden himself. To stylise, or bring something into form, is the basis of human consciousness and the starting point of history. History is always about patterns. I paraphrase the words here of the writer and jazz critic Albert Murray. They bring me back to Marc Rossignol, and how he approaches performance as a transition from ritual into art. Man and play. The ritual visualizes the metaphor. Can these words make one dizzy? "Once you get into art, you are into vertigo." Marc Albert Murray Rossignol. Albert Marc Rossignol Murray. The world is a painting.

It sounds too heroic, now that I reread it: it is another paragraph from the speech. Back then, in 2017, I was reading texts by the music critic, essayist and writer Albert Murray (1916–2013). And still the dizziness remains, even if the world is not a painting, a canvas onto which anything

1
Marc Rossignol, e-mail to the author, May 11th, 2021.

can be projected. What fascinates me to this day is the relationship to painting in Marc Rossignol's practice. The attention to the flowing role of creating, sharing, and passing something on. The 'dizziness' does not occur out of the blue, and, perhaps surprisingly, the use of this word does not have that much to do with looking at Marc Rossignol's paintings. Or, better still, it is not an effect or a result of looking. From art back into ritual: that's more like it. The connection between art and the origin of rituals is another way of pursuing this line of thought.

What if we (again) approach it from a more anthropological (and hence the word) angle: "Another more anthropological definition of art is an elegant extension, celebration, and refinement of the rituals which re-enact survival technology. When you look at a painting, what you see is a stylisation, but it is also a visual or plastic re-enactment of a ritual, and a ritual is a ceremonial re-enactment of some aspect of the basic survival techniques of a given cultural configuration, which may be an aboriginal tribe or a very highly developed nation, a subcontinent, or even a whole continent." [2]

After a performance, Marc Rossignol said to an interviewer with a smile: "I would have liked for Krishna to have protected us from the bad weather and the rain, but I am too 'Pagan'." It is part of the nature of the game, whether or not one lends credence to rules, and prescriptions of art that have been dictated by the West. When we dare to look beyond the familiar boundaries, maybe we will find a greater refinement of options and approaches.

Albert Murray not only refers to a performative aspect, but lays the emphasis on creating, presenting and producing, over and over again. It is about going from ritual back into a playful way of creating, including improvisation, and personal choices for certain stylistic forms and elegance.

Édouard Marc Glissant Rossignol. *Une nouvelle région du monde* ('A New Region of the World') is the title of a book by Édouard Glissant. Marc Rossignol put a copy of it in my hands in the autumn of 2017 — including a reference to specific pages and passages: Marc Édouard Rossignol Glisssant. On page 31 it says: "Language draws and colours first, and *then it recites*." Glissant writes of the origin of language and of painting, of how every book and painting or representation imposes itself, to seize the moment and cause surprise: "The painting, the painted picture is (...) something isolated, a pause, a citation of details, of which we are happy to select the detail, and so much for the illuminating synthesis (...)." [3]

The world is a representation, a painting. Let us then again seek out the dazzle of countless light variations, the interplay of shadows in the caves, the rhythm and chaos of the universe, with its molecular structures and sources of energy. The anonymity of time lost, united in diversity

2
Albert Murray, *Collected Essays and Memoirs*. New York: The Library of America, 2016, 895.

3
Édouard Glissant, *Une nouvelle région du monde*. Esthétique I. Paris: Gallimard, 2006, 31.

and multiplicity, may bring us to a new region, "to see a new aesthetic, perhaps that of that new region of the world that we find here, all of it here." [4]

4
Ibid, 37

I leaf back through Marc Rossignol's self-published books and again there are the patterns, reproductions, of earlier artworks, such as tiles and abstract geometric formations. The logo of the French newspaper *Libération* is cut out, freedom as a logo multiplied into a new composition, numbers, an oak leaf and *Le Monde*. In 2021 it may seem remarkable that newspapers still dare to use 'grand words' as their (enduring) title. Maybe it is especially strange to encounter this within journalism, the so-called Fourth Estate. The French philosopher Jacques Rancière (1940) says on this subject: "There is a whole series of word plays at the heart of political speech that have replaced the major terms on the billboards or coming out of the loudspeakers of times past. Political activism has taken a turn which moves it closer to certain kinds of artistic intervention. As a consequence, each comes with its own billboard, and its own key words. This has been really visible for a decade or so; it is part of the spirit of the times. We remake an experience of the world outside of the grand syntheses, with little fragments which are shared with art. We could say we practice politics today as Godard practiced filmmaking fifty years ago." [5]

5
Jacques Rancière, "L'enjeu est de parvenir à maintenir du dissensus", Jean-Marc Lalanne, in *Les Inrockuptibles*, 15 February 2021, consulted on 10 May 2021, https://www.lesinrocks.com/cheek/rencontre-avec-jacques-ranciere-lenjeu-est-de-parvenir-a-maintenir-du-dissensus-157314-15-02-2021/

At the same time, I am reminded of what Marc Rossignol writes: "In this work I am studying a kolam, a drawing that women trace in the South of India in front of their doors, on the ground, with rice flour, in order to ward off evil spirits." And, not insignificantly, he then adds: "The one I chose has a continuous trace and is made up of a single line." And, I might add, we are not talking about photography or cinema here, which gives us the truth 24 times per second.

Back to the relationship between art, daily life and rituals: in another mini publication by Marc Rossignol, with the title: *Vie et mort de Cézanne, le contexte* (Life and death of Cézanne, the context) I read: "The genesis of the modern artist, the landscape and the colonisation of Algeria." Upon which follows a detailed biography that cannot be found in its entirety in any museum or archive. Because when your historical perspective is directed in major part by a drawing hand, you obtain a different story, with transcultural cross-connections. The beginning or ending of the first phase is perhaps, from a certain perspective, unspecified. It is about the possibility to navigate 'in' and 'through' contexts.
I think of a feather head-covering, a wigwam, a hut, a car, a sphinx, weavings, a windmill, a castle, pyramids, a building of flats, a new weaving, a ziggurat, a hut, a cave dwelling, a mountain range and time and again there are patterns and a weave. Because beauty, "between the day and its sea of flames," is once again open, wherever it may be. [6]

6
Édouard Glissant, *Le sel noir*. Paris: Editions du Seuil, 1960. Original in French and the final sentence of the poem of *Le premier jour*, translated by the author: "Parmi le jour et son embrasement".

# DRAWING WITH BOTH HANDS

*Marc Rossignol*

I trace networks of continuous lines that invade the space and superimpose themselves in an inextricable tangle. Drawing or painting with both hands simultaneously installs a tension; the activity illuminates both body and mind, and the bodily experience guides the mind, which becomes purely receptive. The concurrent recital of texts, with their own beginnings and endings, add further dimensions of interlacing resonance. The overall experience is physical, for sure, and quite similar to practicing a sport, which corresponds to our intrinsic nature. Yet the simultaneity of practices has a neurological impact too, possibly forging new neural pathways, prompting in the mind an acceptance of the universe as a whole.

During the year 1960–1, when I was six years old, I'd find myself sitting at an inclined desk at school. I'd advance my left elbow, fountain pen in hand, towards the white, porcelain inkpot planted in the desk's heavy wooden top. I'd draw my hand back towards the homework, and apply myself to tracing letters. I'd get discouraged, again and again, as my palm that followed the pen smudged the freshly formed letters.

I'd observe my fellow apprentices, all of them right-handed, to see if I could glean how to correct this untoward outcome of my practice. One day — Eureka! — I began to write the text from right to left like in Arabic, and succeeded in completing the page without a single blotch. Proud as a peacock, I submitted my copy to the teacher.

Sometime later, at the home of a great aunt who had passed away, as I was sitting on the dining room floor, I came across a photograph of the Madonna of Berlin by Petrus Christus in a magazine. It was a shock. Georges Bataille situated the beginning of art to the moment human beings began to create funerary rites. In any case, I knew then that art would become my constant preoccupation. In 1990, I painted 25 continuous lines...

In 1990, on the tarmac of twenty intersections, in gold letters, and in twenty languages using a variety of alphabets, I wrote out the orientations north, east, west and south, thus indicating the four cardinal points. In 1993, I aligned these different languages into a single cross that I painted on the ground in front of Détour Gallery (Namur) during a solo exhibition, and in front of the Centre Jacques Franck (Saint-Gilles, Brussels) for a group show. Working on the ground and indicating spatial orientations are my enduring preoccupations.

The first ambidextrous action took place at factor 44 (Antwerp) in October 2000. Onto a piece of paper affixed to the wall I traced, symmetrically, in charcoal, the letters of the alphabet, all the while chanting their names. As I let each letter occupy the whole surface of the page, I was obliged to superimpose them. I reprised this action on canvas in 2004, at the Halles de Schaerbeek (Brussels), and in thick white chalk on black paper, at Peter Funken Gallery (Berlin).

In 1996, onto the tarmac of a walking path in the Soignes forest in Brussels, I inscribed *Promenade Rossignol*, a snaking, discontinuous line, which corresponded to the movements of the walkers' tibias, granting them permission to pass one another. In 1999 I reiterated this same line on a field of grass with birdseed, and entitled it *Déjeuner sur l'herbe*, during the exhibition « *GROEN LABYRINT* » (Oosterwijk-Westerloo). Since that project, I determined my practice has two essential axes: using both hands simultaneously, and working on the ground.

In 2008, on the floor of La Maison de la culture de Namur, I exhibited two continuous lines. One was inspired by a sandroing from Vanuatu, the other by a Chokwe Lusona; I realised both with cast-offs: the coloured plastic tops of soda bottles. The geographical origin of the drawings, Africa and Oceania respectively, in no way prevents them from appearing very alike. These Eulerian traces — drawn in a single, continuous line — are of great interest to ethno-mathematicians, who see in them the occasion to honour the mathematical faculties of extra-European populations. In 2021, at Second Room in Antwerp, I drew with red ink in one hand and blue ink in the other onto a sheet of paper laid flat on the ground. Left and right; before and after, the line begins (before) where it ends (after). The continuous line I traced from memory on this occasion was a Chokwe lusona, named 'cemetery'. Whilst drawing, I recited, also from memory, *Le chant des âmes retrouvées* ('the song of souls refound') by François Cheng. In doing so, I link Africa to China. This action was repeated at Établissements d'en face (2012), Brussels, at Galérie Vincenz Sala, Paris (2013), at Croxhapox, Ghent (2013), at Galerie Annie Gentils, Antwerp (2013) and at INSTITUT DE CARTON, Brussels (2017). In 2015, in black and white, I drew an Indian kolam (another continuous line) entitled *nœud de Brahma* (Brahman knot), all the while reciting *Appunti per un romanzo sull' immondezza* by Pier Paolo Pasolini, at Galerie Vincenz Sala, Paris (2016), at the Jewish Museum of Brussels (2016), the Academy of Saint Gilles, Brussels (2016) and in marble dust for SOFAM, at the European House of Authors, Brussels (2018).

For the performance *Le Premier Jour*, I recite the poem with this title by Edouard Glissant whilst tracing, in black ink on a paper scroll measuring 10 m × 1 m, the twelve mathematical variations of an Indian kolam named *lotus flower*. To each of the twelve variations, I attribute three properties: a month of the year, a flower, and a bird. I have enacted this performance at La Maison de la Culture de Namur (2017), for SOFAM at the European House of Authors, Brussels (2018), and at Galerie Annie Gentils, Antwerp (2018).

I trace networks of continuous lines that invade the space and superimpose themselves in an inextricable tangle. Drawing or painting with both hands, by rote, simultaneously installs a tension: the activity illuminates both body and mind, and the bodily experience guides the mind, which become purely receptive. The concurrent recital of texts, also by heart, with their own beginnings and endings, adds further dimensions of interlacing resonance. The overall experience is physical, for sure, and quite similar to practicing a sport, which corresponds to our intrinsic nature. Yet this simultaneity of practices has a neurological impact too, possibly forging new neural pathways, prompting in the mind an acceptance of the universe as a whole.

Body and mind find an intense convergence in these vocalisations and the traced enunciations of graphic forms that are not really images, nor writing, as yet, but profoundly linked to the instant in which they are iterated. Through an artistic practice that is more like a sport than a virtue, I dance as much as I draw, from a desire to return to the body its creative competencies. I exhaust the brushes' load of ink along the traces, signalling the course, from start to finish. As such, I wish to underscore a particular relationship to the fluid motion of time.

from left to right,
top down:

Sans titre
1990, 220 × 180 cm

Saint-Gilles, 1990

Centre culturel Jacques
Franck, Saint-Gilles, 1993

—

*Alphabetart*
2004

*Promenade Rossignol*
Forêt de Soignes
Brussels, 1996

*Déjeuner sur l'herbe*
1999

—

*À deux mains*
(collection J. Thompson)
2000

Maison de la Culture,
Namur, 2008

Sofam, Brussels, 2018

—

Maison de la Culture,
Namur, 2017

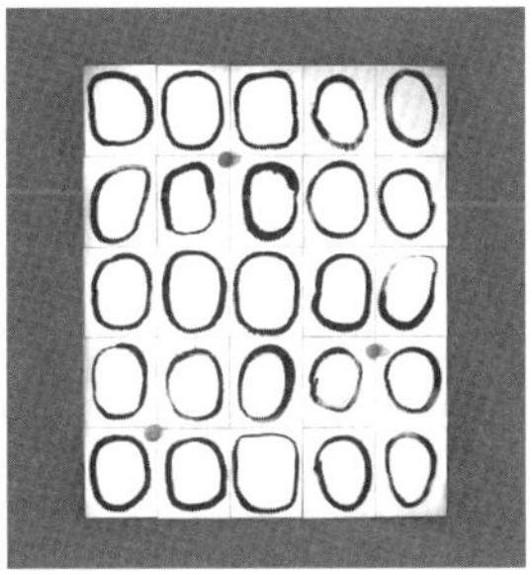

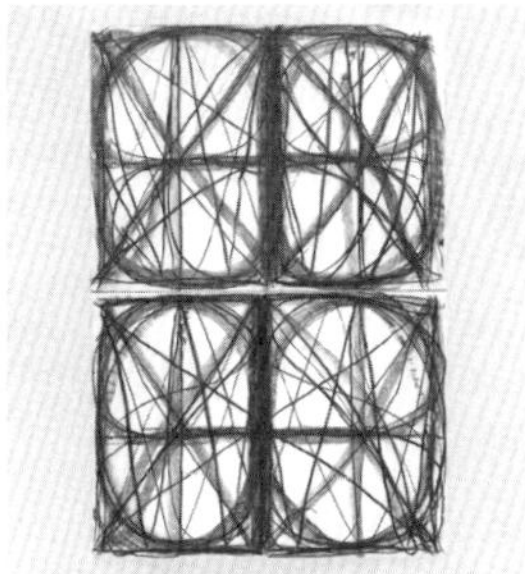

*Special thanks to Annie Gentils*

MER., imprint of Borgerhoff & Lamberigts
www.merbooks.be

ISBN 9789463935241
D/2021/11.089/58



Authors
Kate Christina Mayne
Marc Rossignol
Phillip Van den Bossche

Translation
Kate Christina Mayne

Graphic design
Luc Derycke & Pauline Scharmann, in conversation with Annick Houyet and Marc Rossignol

Photography
Ben Van den Berghe, We Document Art (p. 5–15, 17–19, 21–46, 48–52, 54–55, 57–65, 67–81, 84, 88, 92).
Annick Houyet (p. 85, 89, 98, 101–102). André Goldberg (p. 86). Carine Demeter (p. 87).
Alain Van Caulaert (p. 94). Marc Rossignol (p. 16, 47, 52, 83, 93, 95). Toni Geirlandt (p. 97).
Annie Gentils (p. 99, 105). Nabyl Boutros (p. 100). Dominique Thirion (p. 103).

Vlaanderen
verbeelding werkt